A Note to Parents an

The *Dorling Kindersley Readers* series is a compelling reading program, designed in conjunction with leading literacy experts, including Dr. Linda Gambrell, Director of the School of Education at Clemson University. Dr Gambrell has served on the Board of Directors of the International Reading Association and as President of the National Reading Conference.

The series combines a highly visual approach with engaging, easy-to-read text. Each Reader is guaranteed to capture a child's interest while developing his or her reading skills, general knowledge, and love of reading.

The four levels of Readers are aimed at different reading abilities, enabling you to choose the books that are exactly right for your children:

Level 1—Beginning to Read
Level 2—Beginning to Read Alone
Level 3—Reading Alone
Level 4—Proficient Readers

The "normal" age at which a child begins to read can be anywhere from three to eight years old, so these levels are intended only as a general guideline.

No matter which level you select, you can be sure that you are helping your child learn to read, then read to learn!

Dorling **DK** Kindersley

LONDON, NEW YORK, SYDNEY, DELHI, PARIS,
MUNICH, and JOHANNESBURG

Produced by
Shoreline Publishing Group
Editorial Director James Buckley, Jr.
Art Director Tom Carling, Carling Design Inc.
Creative Consultant Thomas M. Buckley

For Dorling Kindersley Publishing
Senior Editor Cynthia O'Neill
Senior Managing Art Editor Cathy Tincknell
DTP Designer Andrew O'Brien
Production Nicola Torode
US Editor Gary Werner

Reading Consultant Linda Gambrell PhD

First American Edition, 2000

00 01 02 03 04 05 10 9 8 7 6 5 4 3 2 1

Published in the United States by
Dorling Kindersley Publishing, Inc.
95 Madison Ave., New York, New York 10016

pb: ISBN 0-7894-6695-3   hc: ISBN 0-7894-6694-5

Library of Congress Cataloguing-in-Publication Data

Teitelbaum, Michael.
  Creating the X-men: how comic books come to life / by
    Michael Teitelbaum.
    p. cm. -- (Dorling Kindersley readers)
  ISBN 0-7894-6694-5 – ISBN 0-7894-6695-3 (pbk.)
  1. X-men (Comic strip) -- Juvenile literature. [1. X-men (Comic strip)
  2. X-Men (Fictitious characters) 3. Cartoons and comics -- History and
    criticism] I. Title. II Series.

PN6728.X2 T453 2000
741.5'973--dc21
                                         00-034054

Special thanks to Mike Stewart, Chris Claremont,
Adam Kubert, Tim Townsend, Paul Tutrone, and Chris
Dickey for their assistance in making this book.

Printed and bound by L Rex, China

Photography credits:
t=top, b=below, l=left, r=right, c=center,
David Drapkin: 14b, 21b, 26t, 37b, 41b, 46b; **Dorling
Kindersley:** 4tl, 20tl, 22bl, 25br, 30tl, 31c, 35tr; **Stan Lee
Media:** 7b; **Susan Skarr/Courtesy Jack Kirby Estate:** 8b.

see our complete
catalog at
www.dk.com

Contents

DORLING KINDERSLEY *READERS*

PROFICIENT
4
READERS

CREATING THE
X-MEN
HOW COMIC BOOKS
COME TO LIFE

Written by James Buckley, Jr.

A Dorling Kindersley Book

Starts with an X!

People have used pictures to tell stories since prehistoric times, when the first artists painted on the walls of caves.

Of course, things have changed quite a bit since then.

Today, comic books are one of the most popular ways that people tell stories with pictures. The books are made by teams of talented people.

Early art
Prehistoric humans painted pictures of the animals that they hunted. They used paint made from plants.

Over the years, dozens of Super Heroes have joined the X-Men, using their incredible powers to help other people.

Artists, writers, and others work together to bring their stories to readers around the world.

Many of the stories in comic books are about fantastic Super Heroes with amazing powers. One of the most popular Super Hero groups is the X-Men. X-Men comic books describe the adventures of a group of extraordinary people who use their abilities to battle evil beings and save the world.

Each month, X-Men comics are produced by the team at Marvel Comics, a company based in New York City.

It takes many steps to go from the team's imagination to newsstands and comic books stores. This book describes those steps in detail. It takes you inside the world of comic books to meet the artists who create them.

First issue
This first issue of *The X-Men* was published in September 1963.

The first comic books appeared in the 1930s. Some were about Super Heroes, but others featured detectives, cowboys, secret agents, or science fiction. Romance was another popular subject.

Bad guy
From the start, the X-Men's greatest enemy has been the evil mutant Magneto.

Fantastic Four
Meet the Thing, Invisible Girl, Mr. Fantastic, and the Human Torch.

Idea men

Before X-Men comic books could be created, the X-Men themselves had to be thought up.

Writer Stan Lee and artist Jack Kirby were the two people most responsible for creating the X-Men. In fact, Lee and Kirby probably helped create more comic-book Super Heroes than anyone else in the comics industry.

Before they created the X-Men, they dreamed up another Super Hero group, the Fantastic Four.

The X-Men first appeared in 1963. Later on, Lee and Kirby wrote and drew the Avengers, the incredible Hulk, and the mighty Thor.

For the X-Men, the pair came up with the idea of a team of teenage mutants being taught by Professor Charles Xavier.

Mutants are living creatures, in this case human beings, whose genes are changed in some important way. In the case of the X-Men, their altered genes give them superpowers.

Lee at first wanted to call the team "The Mutants," but Marvel executives thought that young readers might not know what mutants were.

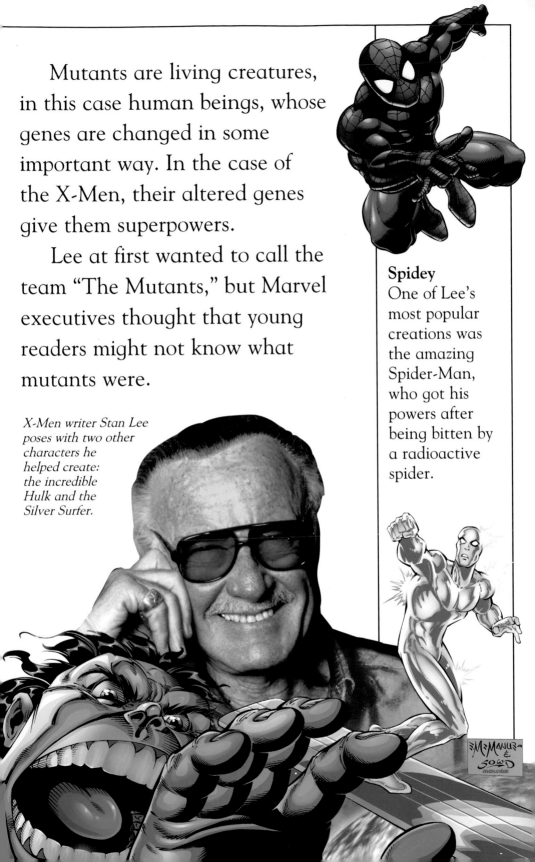

X-Men writer Stan Lee poses with two other characters he helped create: the incredible Hulk and the Silver Surfer.

Spidey
One of Lee's most popular creations was the amazing Spider-Man, who got his powers after being bitten by a radioactive spider.

Danger Room
This high-tech room was a safe, secure place where the X-Men could practice their skills.

Lee invented the name "X-Men" and he wrote the story for the first issue. Kirby, one of the greatest artists in comics history, drew the first X-Men.

"Jack was the best guy to work with," Lee said. "Any idea I gave him, he would make better. It was Jack's idea to open the first issue in the Danger Room."

"Cap"
During World War II (1939–1945), Kirby helped create the patriotic hero Captain America (who became known as "Cap" for short).

Jack Kirby's style influenced generations of other artists.

Kirby had been a comics artist for decades when he teamed up with Lee at Marvel. He had worked on many Super Hero, Western, and monster comic books for several companies.

For the first X-Men comic book, Kirby created pencil drawings for each panel of each page. He created the look of each character, and expanded and refined Lee's story. Later, these drawings were traced over with black ink and colored up.

Lee had been a part of Marvel since 1940, when it was known as Timely Comics. Lee, the nephew of company founder Martin Goodman, joined as an office assistant and moved quickly into writing. By the time he was 20 years old, he was the company's editor and chief writer.

Angel
This high-flying member of the X-Men shows Kirby's style when he first drew the team in 1963.

Before X-Men
Marvel comic books in the 1940s featured Super Heroes and many other characters.

There have been many X-Men comic book series, including The Uncanny X-Men and X-Men: The Hidden Years.

The first
An earlier version of the Human Torch was featured on the first *Marvel Comics* cover in 1939.

Over the next decade, Marvel helped make comic books enormously popular. Lee, and his fellow Marvel writers and editors, changed the way that readers thought of comics. Before then, heroes were always perfect and more than human. But Marvel Super Heroes were ordinary people with extraordinary powers.

Working with Kirby and others, Lee developed the "Marvel Method" of creating comics. In this method, the writer creates the plot of each comic book. The artist draws panels that tell the writer's story in pictures. The writer then comes up with the words the characters say or think.

This unique teamwork helped revolutionize how comic books are created. The artist is as much a part of the storytelling as the writer.

Today, the X-Men appear in several of the most popular comic book series in the world. Dozens of new heroes have joined the team.

On the next two pages you'll find a special X-Men comic sample.

In this book, you'll read about how Marvel created these pages of X-Men action!

Now and then
The look of a character can change greatly when drawn by different artists. Artistic styles change over time, too. Compare the Beast today (*above*) with his look in 1963 (*below*).

Story: MIKE STEWART   Pencils: ANTHONY WILLIAMS   Inks: DAN PANOSIAN   Colors: CHRIS DICKEY   Letters: PAUL TUTRONE
Editor: MARK POWERS   Editor in Chief: BOB HARRAS

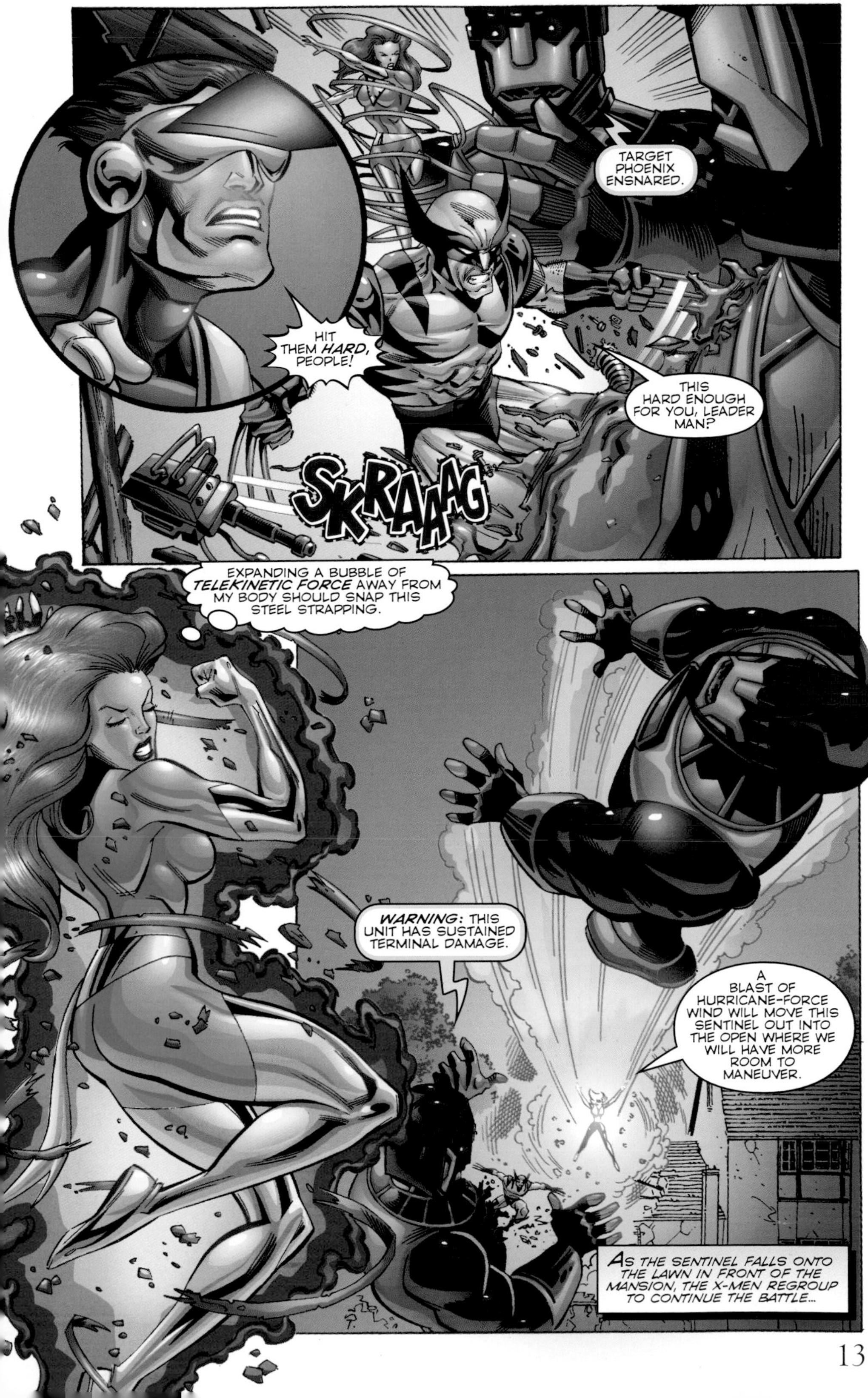
HIT THEM HARD, PEOPLE!
TARGET PHOENIX ENSNARED.
THIS HARD ENOUGH FOR YOU, LEADER MAN?
SKRAAAG
EXPANDING A BUBBLE OF TELEKINETIC FORCE AWAY FROM MY BODY SHOULD SNAP THIS STEEL STRAPPING.
WARNING: THIS UNIT HAS SUSTAINED TERMINAL DAMAGE.
A BLAST OF HURRICANE-FORCE WIND WILL MOVE THIS SENTINEL OUT INTO THE OPEN WHERE WE WILL HAVE MORE ROOM TO MANEUVER.
AS THE SENTINEL FALLS ONTO THE LAWN IN FRONT OF THE MANSION, THE X-MEN REGROUP TO CONTINUE THE BATTLE...

Words come first

The first step in creating the X-Men action scene on the previous pages involved not pictures, but words.

One of the best-known comic book writers is Chris Claremont. Along with being a writer, Chris is the editorial director at Marvel, overseeing the work of other editors and writers.

3-16-00

PAGE ONE

SPLASH of two SENTINELS cr
X-men's mansion headquarter
the roof of the mansion like
reaches in, threateningly, tryin
their home turf with determi

Check your spelling
An editor is part of the team that creates comic books. He or she uses special marks like these (in red) to correct a writer's script or plot.

Chris Claremont started at Marvel in 1968. He has written for The Fantastic Four, Uncanny X-Men, Wolverine, *and many others.*

Writers at Marvel create stories that include plot and action, but don't always include dialogue, which is the name for the words that the characters speak.

A comic book artist called a "penciler" takes the story by Chris and creates the pictures. Chris adds the dialogue later.

"My main responsibility as the writer is to tell the story to the artist in a clear and precise way," Chris says. "The artist turns around and tells that story, using pictures."

In the "Marvel Method," Chris says, the writer first tells the story using "narrative." This is the kind of style that you might read in a novel.

"I create the who, what, when, where, and how," Chris says. "Who is in each scene? What are they doing? Where are they?"

More bad guys
Sentinels, the villains on pages 12–13, are evil robots who battle the X-Men.

Chris's first
Chris began writing for the X-Men in 1974 with this important issue, *X-Men #94*.

To write that story, Chris uses a style specific to comic books.

"As the writer, you have to think visually," he said. "Everything that goes on to the comic page is the writer's responsibility. What are the characters wearing? What is their body language saying about them? What kind of rooms or settings are they in?"

"You are creating this world for the artist and the reader. And you have to do this in pictures. You want to give the artist as much information as possible."

"You have to help the artist create powerful pictures, and give him ideas that will inspire his imagination."

For instance, Chris would not simply write, "Then Cyclops fights Magneto."

He would write a more detailed description of the battle.

The relationship between the writer and the artist is an important one in creating comic books. As you will see, creating comic books takes a lot of teamwork.

This is a page from the story that was used to create the action scene on pages 12–13.

Words to pictures
Read the story page below and see how the artist took the writer's words and turned them into the pictures on pages 12–13. Can you find each sentence in the drawing?

"Suddenly...The Sentinels!"
Plot for 2 Pages
3-16-00

<u>PAGE ONE</u>

SPLASH of two SENTINELS crashing through the side of the X-Men's mansion headquarters. One Sentinel has ripped open the roof of the mansion like the lid of a box. The second reaches in, threateningly, trying to grab Cyclops. Defending their home turf with determination, the X-Men hit their robotic attackers hard. Cyclops unleashes his optic blast on the hand of his attacker. Wolverine dives at the torso of the same Sentinel breaking open the roof. Phoenix hurls a jagged, broken timber from the roof through the torso of this Sentinel with her telekinesis.

Title, Credits and Indicia should go on this page.

<u>PAGE TWO</u>

Close on Cyclops as he unleashes another optic blast and shouts orders to the team.

Reverse angle as Wolverine lands on his Sentinel and tears into it with his claws, disabling the robot. In the background we can see the other Sentinel firing constrictive metal tentacles out of his hand, capturing Phoenix.

17

THIS HARD ENOUGH FOR YOU, LEADER MAN?

Word up
Words the characters say or think are placed into spaces or shapes called balloons.

Phoenix
One of the original X-Men, her real name is Jean Grey. She has incredible mental powers.

After the artist has delivered the penciled art, Chris, as the writer, completes his work by writing the dialogue.

Chris draws on a photocopy of the pencils to show where he wants to place the "balloons" that hold the dialogue. He provides a printout of the dialogue to the letterer.

"Sometimes the art will come back and not be exactly what I expected," Chris says. "So I might have to rewrite some dialogue to match the art."

This demonstrates an important point Chris makes about the comic book creation process.

"It requires a lot of flexibility," he says. "You have to be ready to deal with all sorts of unexpected problems at every stage of the process."

| 6 | Wolverine: | Who cares how they got in, Jeannie. Point is, we gotta send 'em back out again—in pieces! |
| 7 | SFX: | Zrak |

PAGE TWO

1	Cyclops:	Hit them hard, people!
2	Sentinel:	Target Phoenix ensnared
3	SFX:	Skraag
4	Wolverine:	This hard enough for you, leader man?
5	Phoenix: (thought)	Expanding a bubble of telekinetic force away from my body should snap this steel strapping.

This shows how the writer created dialogue for pages 12-13.

To prepare to be a writer, Chris suggests that you do plenty of reading.

"And don't just read comic books," he says. "Read fiction, read history, read as much as you can."

"Watch the world around you. Watch and learn about people and how they move and act and speak."

"The more you know and the more you learn, the more you will have available to you to include in your stories."

Professor X
Professor Charles Xavier gathered the X-Men from around the world to form them into a team to help others.

19

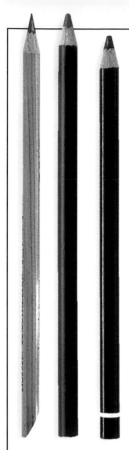

Tools of the trade
Artists choose different kinds of pencils to change the look of a drawing. For example, a sharp, hard pencil makes for a crisp outline on the page while thicker, softer pencil lines add texture.

People who "pencil"

In comic books, a pencil is not just something you draw with...it's an action, too.

Artists called "pencilers" use special lead pencils to draw comic books. After the writer has written the plot, the penciler draws the entire story.

This process, which is called "penciling," is unique to comic books. Penciling means the process of drawing all the characters, action, and backgrounds in each panel of a comic book.

This step in the making of a comic book is as much a part of the storytelling as the writing.

"The most important job for a penciler is to tell the story," says longtime X-Men artist Adam Kubert. "If the reader can't follow the story, then it's not a story, it's just a bunch of pretty pictures."

Adam has been with Marvel since 1994. His father, Joe, is a respected comic book artist and runs an art school, too.

"I grew up around comic books," Adam says. "That was dinner-table conversation for us."

Hard at work
In his studio, Adam works on a tilted drawing table. He is surrounded by models and reference materials for his drawings, as well as practice sketches.

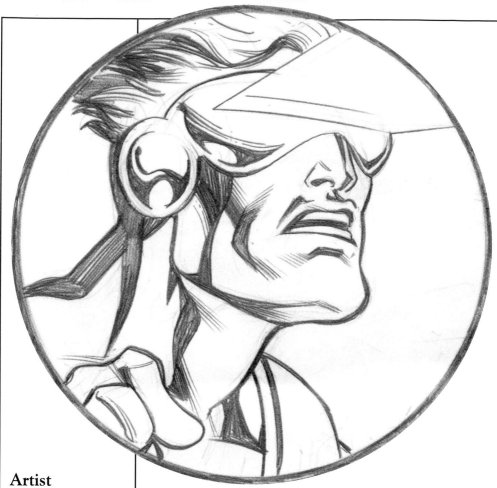

To make this picture of Cyclops look more three-dimensional, the artist drew some heavier lines, to create shadows.

Artist meets doctor Medical illustrators are trained to draw exact replicas of the human body and its parts.

Adam studied medical illustration in college, but decided that drawing fictional characters would be more fun than drawing real people. He enrolled in his father's art school to study comic book art. After graduating, he began working in comic books.

Adam says pencilers begin by reading the plot several times.

"Then I figure out where to put the emphasis in each part of the story," he says.

Pencilers also decide what size the panels will be. Different-sized panels make some parts of the action more important than others.

Look again at pages 12–13. The left page is one giant action-packed panel. On the right page, three panels build up the drama, with the largest panel at the end.

The penciler also added drama by making the Sentinel fly toward the reader. This makes for a more exciting scene than if the figure shot to the rear of the picture.

Panels
Each smaller section of a comic book page is called a panel. They can be almost any shape or size that the artist chooses.

Grrrr!
Artists create emotion in characters with a few pencil strokes. How do you think Wolverine is feeling here?

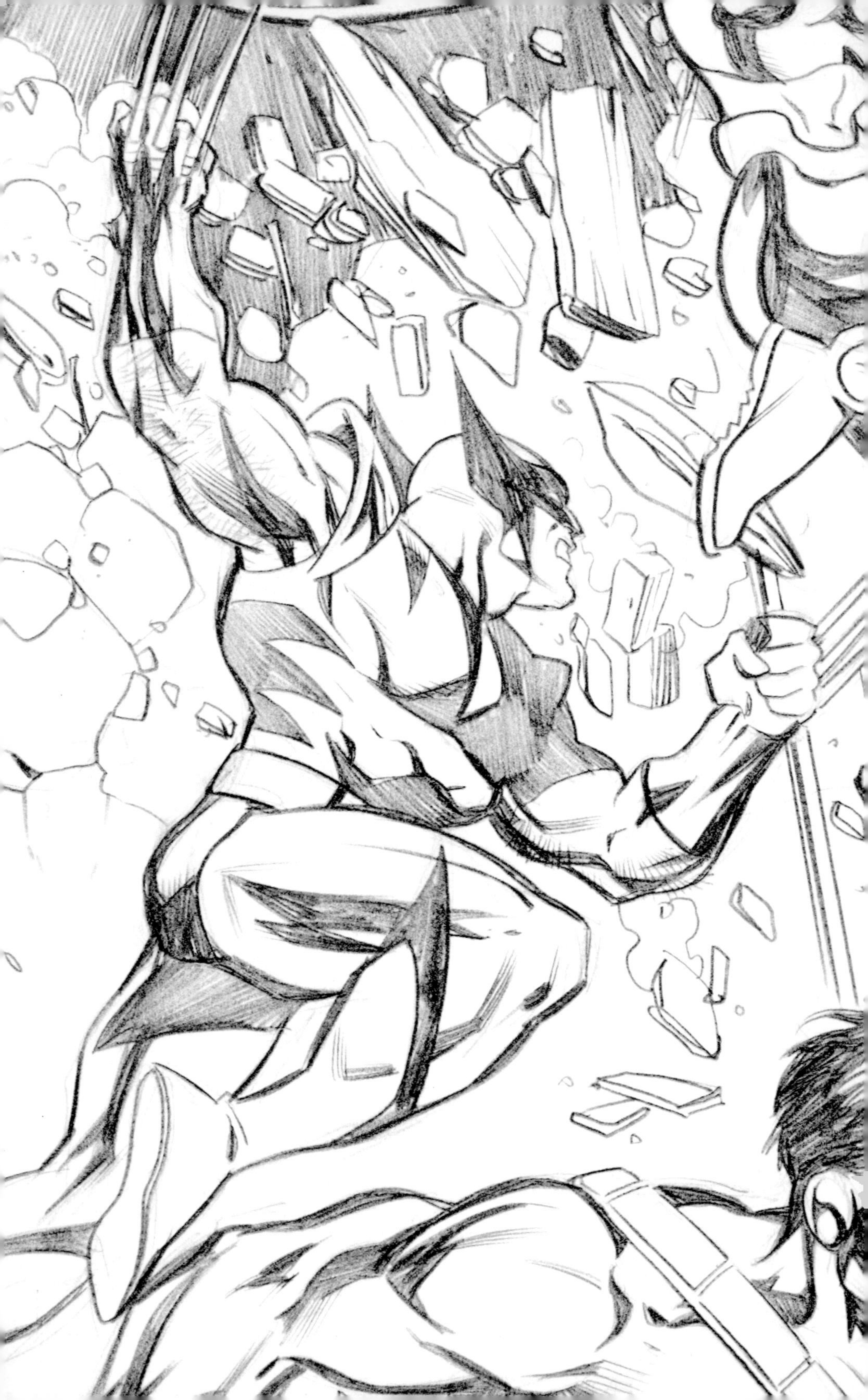

"Once the decisions about panels are made, I "rough out" the first seven pages or so," Adam says.

Adam sketches boxes on each page, representing final panels. Then he roughs out a quick version of the action. Outline drawings of the characters come next.

During all of this work, Adam is constantly revising and changing.

"What is so much fun about penciling is taking chances and trying new ideas," he says. "The nice thing about pencils is what is at the other end...an eraser!"

Adam also is in constant contact with other members of the team.

"Sometimes what works in the written word just doesn't translate to pictures," he says. "So the writer and I talk about another approach. The whole process is a team effort."

Test your own penciling skills. Use this page as a guide to draw Wolverine attacking the Sentinels. Practice using different kinds of line and shading.

On board
Adam draws on heavy art boards such as this one, each measuring 11 x 17 in.

Mistake saver
White plastic erasers are best for pencil drawing. They are firm and do not rub away the surface of the paper.

Dress up
Pencilers create the costumes that characters wear. It is important that the costumes of X-Men, such as Colossus (*below*), remain exactly the same from page to page and from issue to issue.

While everyone has a hand in the process, it is Adam who makes the characters come alive. From buildings to trees to vehicles, the penciler draws everything that the reader sees.

Drawing the X-Men characters is the biggest part of his job.

Using his artistic training, and many hours of practice, Adam now can draw each character from any angle and showing any emotion.

"It takes time to become familiar with the characters," he says.

On staff
Marvel staff members work in offices decorated with comic book art. More than 150 men and women work to produce more than 50 different comic books each month.

"You need to be able to show them in any situation."

Adam also must keep in mind the story, the action, the flow of the reader's eye across the page, and, of course, the quality of the drawing.

Busy work
This detail shows just how much the penciler has to draw, from large hands to bits of debris.

"I like to compare it to making movies," Adam says. "But I'm the director, the makeup artist, the fashion designer, the set designer, everything."

Logo
The title of the comic, which appears on the top of the cover, is called a logo.

Hands down
Even things as simple as hands takes many hours of practice and years of study to draw correctly.

Along with using reference materials for the characters, Adam does other research.

"For instance, we did a scene set in Russia," he says. "So I looked at pictures of buildings there to make my art look as authentic as possible.

"I also do a lot of research on fashion. After all, what the X-Men wear isn't what I wear every day!"

One of Adam's most important roles is to help create the cover of each comic book he draws.

"The cover is the icing on the cake," he says. "I normally do the cover somewhere in the middle of the process."

"We're trying to sell the book with the cover. So we do some things differently than inside. We have to leave room for the logo, the computer bar code, and for cover lettering and titles."

"If there's a scene inside the issue that works on the cover, I adapt that. If not, we create a sort of mini-poster."

"The cover image needs to have action, movement, and involve key characters, while also being eye-catching."

It takes 20 to 25 days from the time Adam receives the script to the time he finishes. But he wouldn't do any other job.

"I couldn't do this for ten or twelve hours a day, six days a week, if I didn't enjoy it. I know I'm lucky. I'm doing what I love to do," he says.

Pay up
The "bar code" in the bottom right-hand corner is used by special scanners at comic book stores to record the price.

Florida?
Marvel artists don't all live in New York. Many, like Tim, work in other towns and mail their work in to Marvel.

In the ink
Thick black ink is used to draw over the work of the penciler. Artists use different brands, but most are based on India ink.

Inside inking

As a Marvel penciler finishes each page of his pencil drawings, he sends them to another artist, such as Tim Townsend at his studio in Florida.

Tim is a special kind of artist called an "inker." The lines drawn by the penciler are not strong enough to print from, so the inker goes over the lines with thick, black ink.

But there is much more to inking than tracing the penciled lines.

"I use ink to give the drawing depth, mood, and texture," Tim says. "An inker is every bit as much an artist as the penciler. I think of it like creating a building."

"The writer is the architect; he does the plans. The penciler is the carpenter; he makes the frame. The inker puts in the walls, the floors, the windows, and everything else."

Tim begins by drawing around the edges of all the panels. He uses a pen and plastic triangles to make sure the lines are very straight.

Ink man
Tim started his art career when he was four years old by tracing over comic books. He later studied art and design in high school and college.

Tools of the trade
Inkers use pens with special tips, called "nibs," to create different kinds of line. Some nibs produce very thin, delicate lines. Other nibs make thick marks.

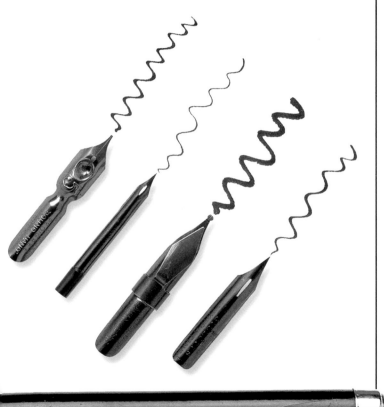

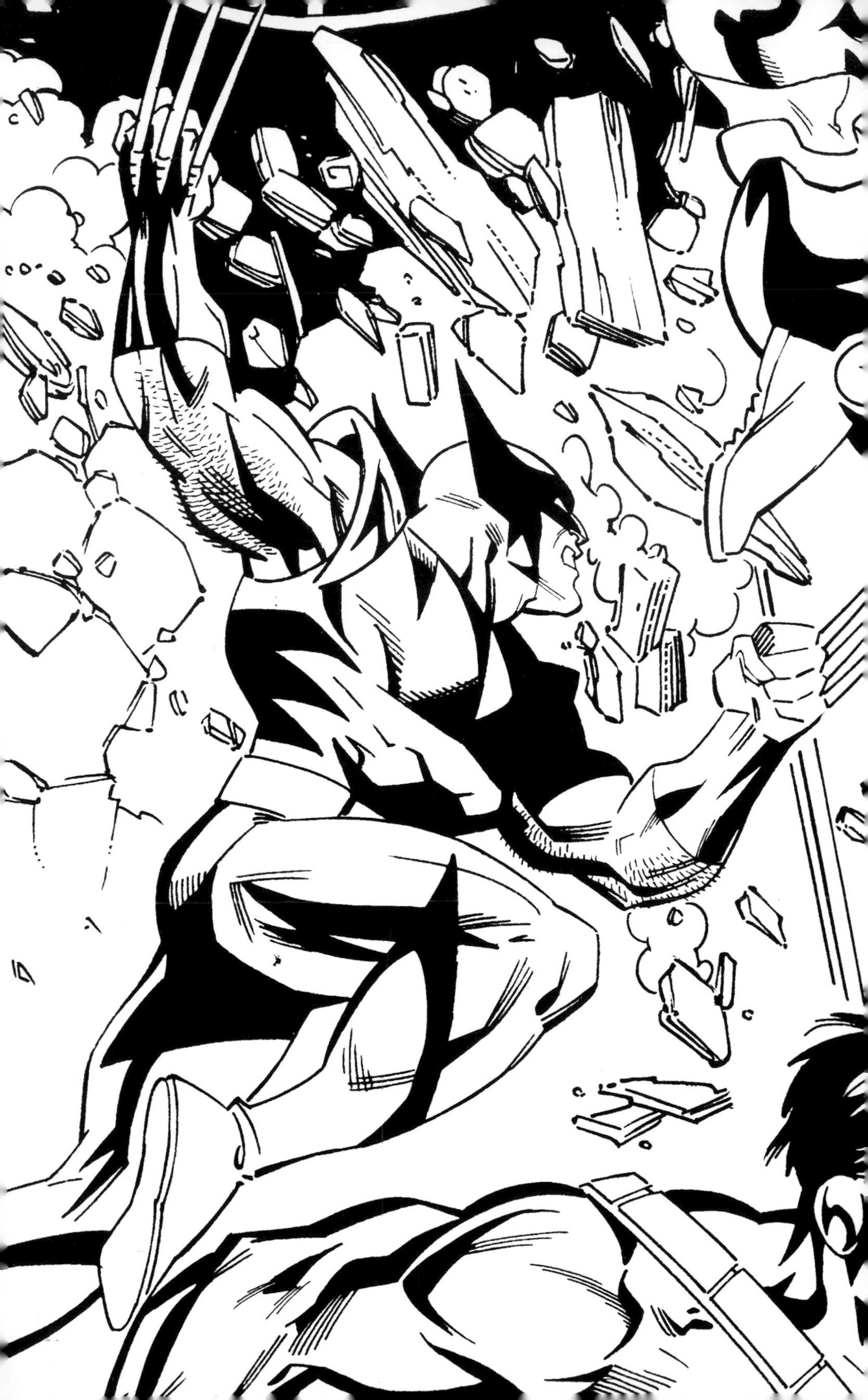

Tim then moves on to inking each figure in each panel, along with the vehicles, buildings, settings, and background.

"Every line you see is one that an inker put there," he says.

However, as with everything else in comic book creation, this is a group effort. Tim and Marvel pencilers work closely together to make sure their vision of the page comes to life.

"The penciler relies on the inker to maintain the vision while also interpreting it in ink," Tim says.

After he has finished inking a page, Tim erases any remaining pencil lines. Tim can finish inking about a page a day, which means it takes him about a month to produce a complete issue of *X-Men*.

Seen this before? Check out page 24. This is the inked version of that page. Notice how the black ink makes Wolverine look more powerful.

Different strokes
Compare these two drawings of Bishop, a tough and powerful member of the X-Men, to see how different inkers use their own style of inking.

Inkers such as Tim use many special techniques to make figures and action come to life.

"I have to make art on a flat page seem three-dimensional," Tim says. "I use ink and line to help fool the reader's eye."

For instance, thick lines appear to be closer to the viewer than thin lines. So figures in the foreground often are created using thicker lines.

Another technique Tim uses is called "cross-hatching." He uses a series of lines that cross over each other. This method creates the illusion of different "shades" of black.

"Black ink is black," Tim says.

Details
See how the inker used many thin, dark lines to make these fingers look rounded. The heaviest block of dark ink forms the shape of the hand itself.

Inkers use plastic triangles as straight edges to draw panels and other lines.

"There are no grays. But cross-hatching can make a black area appear lighter or darker, depending on the amount of lines you use."

Tim uses cross-hatching to help heads and bodies appear round and to give a scene depth.

Using all this thick black ink, does Tim ever worry about making mistakes?

"Inkers never make mistakes," he says with a laugh. "But if we do, we just use regular old white-out."

Tim is another example of an artist who has loved comic books his whole life.

"This is the kind of work I've always wanted to do," he says.

Dark and light
The sun is coming from the upper left in this scene. We can tell this because the inker used only a little ink on the Sentinel with his face to the sun. However, to show that the lower face is in shadow, the inker added thick ink lines.

Keyboard to success
Once, letterers like Paul Tutrone wrote dialogue by hand. Today they work on computers. Paul positions the balloons using the computer mouse.

Letter perfect

While the inker completes his work, the writer is working at the same time to create the script. This is the name for the dialogue that the writer creates to go with the action, after the penciler has finished drawing the panels.

The writer uses photocopies of the penciled artwork as a guide. He writes the words that characters say. He also writes the text that will appear in boxes or as sound effects. He sketches "balloons" into which those words will go.

A letterer, such as Paul Tutrone, then puts those words into place on the actual comic book page.

"We combine the words the writer has created with the page created by the penciler and the inker," Paul says.

First, Paul turns the inked pages into computer files. Then he places balloons throughout the page. The words for each balloon or box are then typed into the file.

Paul works from the script, fitting speech into a balloon.

Balloons
Spaces containing words are called balloons. Straight lines around the balloon edge indicate that words are said out loud; wavy lines show that the words are thoughts.

Font
A font is an individually designed alphabet used in printing. This book, for instance, uses a font called Goudy.

ZAP! POW!
Dramatic, written sound effects are a big part of comic books' unique look. They add color and impact to a story. Letterers create these effects by hand, then scan them into the page.

Scanning
A scanner takes an electronic picture of a page, then translates it into a file the computer can read.

Tutrone's work has changed quite a bit over his years with Marvel. This is because computers have been added to the process.

"Originally, an artist drew each letter and each balloon by hand with ink," Paul says. "Today computers do that same work."

However, the human touch remains. Artists draw an entire alphabet, as well as all punctuation (commas, quotation marks, etc). Those letters and marks are put into the computer using a machine called a "scanner."

Paul then uses a computer program called Fontographer®. This program, or set of instructions, lets him create a computer "font." That font is then used to make the letters on the comic book page.

"Comic books need to have that hand-created look and feel," he says. "We use computers, but only to save time, not to take the artist's place."

Paul's work as a letterer may not seem like an art, but it is. He studied art, design, and typography, which is the art of using words in design. He uses these skills to place balloons properly on the page.

Without letterers, comic books would be very "quiet" places!

TARGET PHOENIX ENSNARED.

Robot talk
Balloons can be printed in colors or shapes to show different "sounds," such as the Sentinels' robotic tone.

Italics
A letterer can use *italic* letters to show that some words in a sentence are more important than others, as happens in this thought bubble.

EXPANDING A BUBBLE OF *TELEKINETIC FORCE* AWAY FROM MY BODY SHOULD SNAP THIS STEEL STRAPPING.

Color their world

Up to this point, the only colors in the X-Men scene are black and white. Now it's time to add color.

The coloring stage is where art and technology meet. Artists, such as Marvel's Chris Dickey, combine a knowledge of art and color with computer expertise.

First, a little history lesson. Until computers made the job faster and easier, colorists worked with dyes and markers and brushes. They carefully colored the inked pages and sent the results to craftworkers called color separators.

These people used very sharp knives to cut out blocks of special color film, called acetate. The blocks matched the paint and dye shades on the colored page.

Think ink
Comic book artists formerly used inks such as these on paper. Today, the colorful ink isn't in pens, but in the hi-tech presses that actually print the books.

Hey, Mac!
Chris used a computer called an Apple Macintosh® G3 to add the colors onto the comic pages. Many comic book workers use Macintosh computers.

The comic book pages were printed using that color film.

"The computer changed all that," Dickey says. "Now we choose colors for every part of the page and the computer colors them in."

Dickey receives the inked page from the editor. He scans this page into a computer file.

Using a program called Adobe Photoshop®, he assigns colors to every part of the pages.

One color
The first comic books were black and white. This was because they had started out as newspaper comic strips, before they were gathered into book form.

Colorful desk
Chris keeps color guides handy at the side of his desk. It helps him to ensure he creates colors accurately.

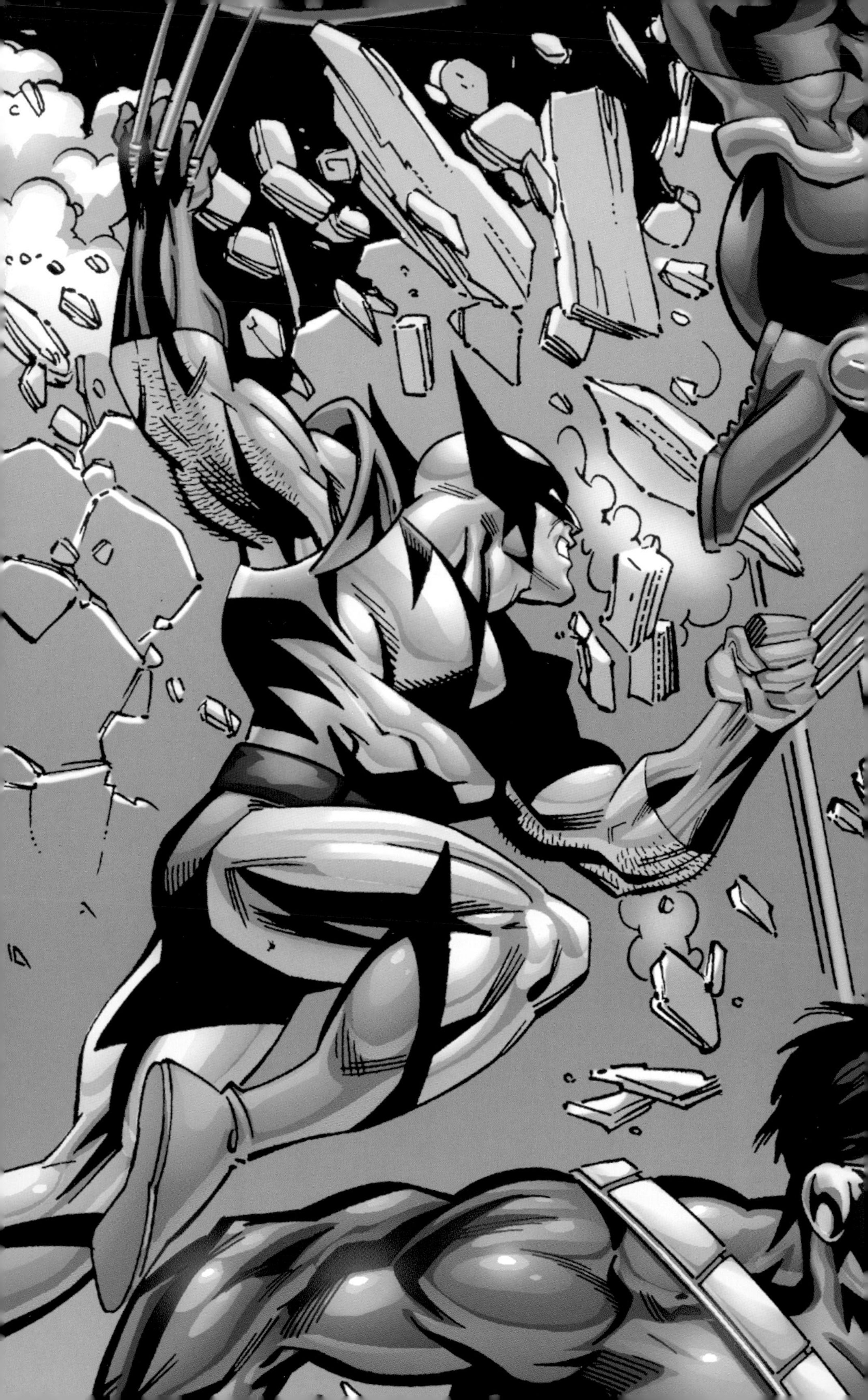

This process is not just color by numbers, however. Every scene has different challenges and might contain many individual areas to color.

Also, the characters' costumes can appear slightly different from panel to panel. For example, Wolverine's costume will be brighter in sunlight, and darker in shade.

"The colorist should understand how light should be shown in the art," Chris says.

Colorists completely fill the panels with color; there is not very much white space in comic books.

"Like pencilers, we have our own styles," Chris says. "You can look at a page that I've colored and, if you're a fan, know it's my work right away. I can do the same looking at other colorists' work."

First pencils, then inks, now color: Look back to pages 24 and 32 and compare them to this fully-inked scene. See how all three artists worked together to make Wolverine come to life.

Purple power
As the Sentinel's ray hits Phoenix, see how Chris has used many varieties and shades of purple and pink, rather than just one single purple-colored line. This use of color makes the action more dramatic.

Weather master

Born in Africa, Storm, also called Ororo, is the member of the X-Men team with complete control of the weather. She calls on the wind, lightning, rain, or snow to help her teammates.

The basics

These boxes represent 100 percent versions of each of the basic colors of the CMYK process.

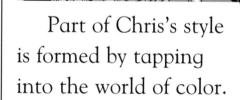

Part of Chris's style is formed by tapping into the world of color.

Comic books, like most printed materials—including this book—are created using a "four-color" printing process. Four pieces of color film are combined to create every color you see on this page...and on every comic book page.

The four colors are cyan (a kind of blue), magenta (a kind of red), yellow, and black. They are abbreviated "CMYK."

For example, to create the exact dark blue needed for Cyclops' uniform, Chris tells the computer to combine different, precise amounts of cyan, magenta, and black. The computer reads this as "100C 60M 15K" to make the uniform the correct dark blue.

"There are literally millions of colors available to us," Dickey says. "In a place where the color goes from light to dark over a small space, thousands of colors can appear in a few inches."

Using the CMYK code, Chris puts the work of Chris Claremont, Adam Kubert, Tim Townsend, and Paul Tutrone into rich, full color.

Color shift
When a color changes from light to dark (or vice versa) in a small space, the shift is called a "gradient." An example is Cyclops' ray, *below.*

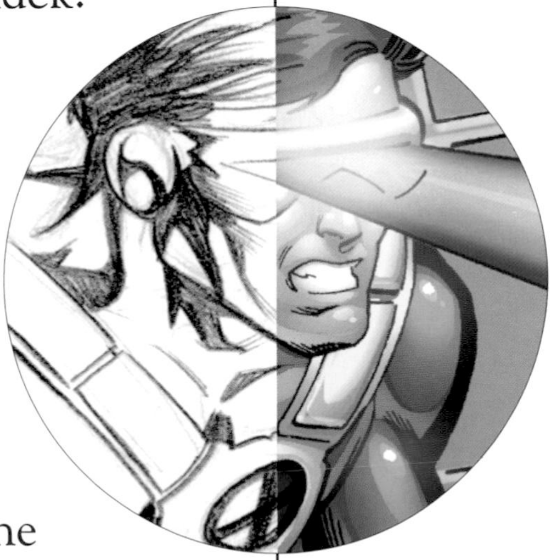

Split screen
See how the original pencil drawing of Cyclops looks with inks and color added in this special side-by-side view.

It's a wrap!

There's one key person left for us to meet. In some ways, perhaps, he is the most important in the creation process: the editor.

Mark Powers has been the editor of X-Men comic books since 1993. He oversees the work of all the people featured in this book. Mark has the ultimate responsibility to see that the comic books come out on schedule.

"I work to keep all the artists on time," he says.

Mark also works with new writers and artists to make sure they learn the "Marvel Method." But while Mark and his team create comic books for a living, it is also a joy. The same is true for all the artists and writers who work at Marvel.

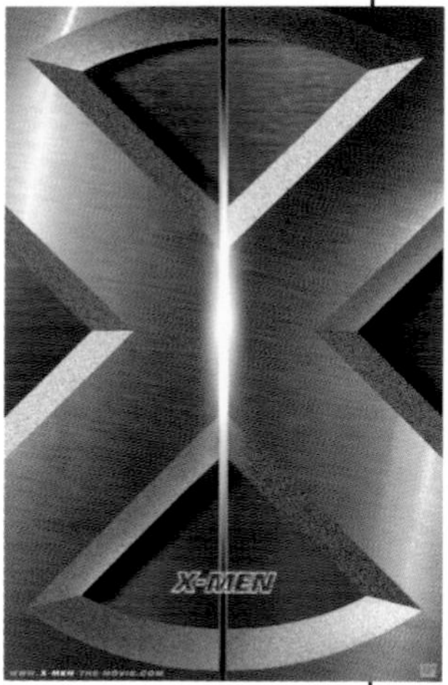
X-MEN

Big screen
The X-Men starred in their first big movie in the summer of 2000.

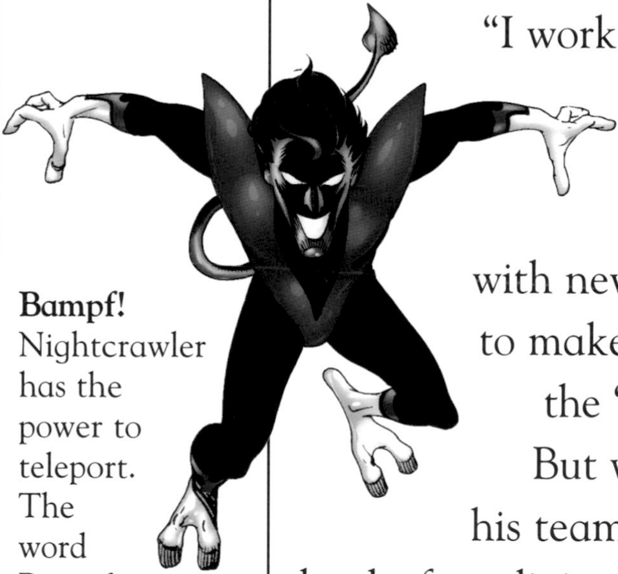

Bampf!
Nightcrawler has the power to teleport. The word Bampf! lets readers know when this happens.

Mark and the rest of the team ensure that X-Men comic books arrive at your store on time each month.

"When I was collecting 30 comic books a month when I was a kid, I never dreamed I'd work at Marvel," Chris Dickey says.

The others in this book agree. For them, creating comic books is a dream come true.

Maybe if it's your dream, it will come true someday, too.

Collect 'em all
One of the ways that fans enjoy comic books is to collect every title of a series.

Icy blast from the past
Iceman was one of the original members of the X-Men.

Glossary

Balloons
In comic books, the spaces in which dialogue or thoughts are shown.

Collaboration
Working with other people on a joint project.

Colorist
In comic books, an artist who places colors onto the inked pages, often using a computer.

CMYK
Abbreviation for "cyan, magenta, yellow, and black," the colors used in the "four-color" printing process.

Cross-hatching
Artistic technique used by inkers, in which many small lines are used to create the illusion of shades of gray, using only black ink.

Dialogue
Words spoken by characters in a comic book, play, book, or screenplay.

Editor
A person who oversees the creation of a comic book and checks all words and pictures for accuracy.

Font
In printing, a set of type in a certain style and size.

Genes
Chemicals inside cells that help create every part of the human body.

Inking
In comic books, the process of putting heavy black ink onto the penciled drawings of each page.

Letterer
In comic books, the artist who creates the actual letters used to show what characters are saying.

Logo
The bold, colorful letters at the top of the front cover of a comic book.

Mutants
Any beings whose gene structure has changed them into a variation of their normal form.

Nibs
Small metal points used on the ends of artists' ink pens—different nibs produce different widths and styles of lines.

Panel
On the comic book page, a space defined by straight lines—most pages have several panels on them.

Pencil
In comic books, a verb describing the first step in the drawing process.

Scan
To use a machine called a scanner, to create an electronic file.

Scene
A small part of a dramatic action, usually set in one place or in the space of a short time.

Script
In comic books, the plot structure and story created by a writer.

Sound effect
In comic books, words that try to show what a particular sound or action sounds like— often drawn in large and colorful ways.

Super Heroes
Fictional characters, often in comic books, with superhuman powers.

Three-dimensional
The appearance of depth, along with height and width, in flat art.